Scratch and Sniff

Margaret Ryan

illustrated by Nathan Reed

A & C Black • London

White Wolves Series Consultant: Sue Ellis,
Centre for Literacy in Primary Education

This book can be used in the White Wolves Guided Reading programme
with children who need a lot of support with reading at Year 3 level

First published 2006 by
A & C Black Publishers Ltd
38 Soho Square, London, W1D 3HB

www.acblack.com

Text copyright © 2006 Margaret Ryan
Illustrations copyright © 2006 Nathan Reed

The rights of Margaret Ryan and Nathan Reed to be identified
as author and illustrator of this work respectively have been
asserted by them in accordance with the Copyrights,
Designs and Patents Act 1988.

ISBN 0-7136-7632-9
ISBN 978-0-7136-7632-7

A CIP catalogue for this book is available from the British Library.

Printed and bound in Great Britain by Bookmarque Ltd, Croydon

Contents

Chapter One   5

Chapter Two   14

Chapter Three   20

Chapter Four   27

Chapter Five   33

About the Author   45

For Tabitha with love

Chapter One

Scratch and Sniff were curled up in the kitchen of Corner Cottage, trying to have a lie-in. But it wasn't easy. Police Constable Penny Penrose was late for work again.

"Has anyone seen my bicycle clips?" she asked.

Scratch scratched, then wandered over to the kitchen door and barked.

"Well done, Scratch," said Penny. She removed the bicycle clips from the door handle and put them on. Then she looked around again.

"Has anyone seen my bicycle helmet?"

Sniff sniffed, then waddled underneath the kitchen table and barked.

"Well done, Sniff," said Penny. She picked up the helmet and put it on. "Now, you boys eat up your breakfast and I'll see you later." Then she hurried outside, jumped on her old bike, and pedalled off to the police station.

Scratch yawned and scratched. Sniff yawned and sniffed.

"Shall we stroll over and check out the food bowls, Sniff?" said Scratch.

"Good idea, Scratch," said Sniff.

But it wasn't.

"Yuk!" said Scratch. "Dried food pellets again."

"What does Penny think we are?" asked Sniff. "Budgies?"

Scratch shook his shaggy, collie head. Sniff rippled his sleek, dachshund body.

It was time for some proper food, they agreed, and headed out through the dog flap to Mrs Pudding's cake shop.

Mrs Pudding was piling up trays with some home baking when they arrived.

"Good morning, boys," she smiled. "Your usual, is it?"

Scratch and Sniff barked and wagged their tails, and then the two of them settled down outside the shop to enjoy their custard buns. They had just got to the squidgy bit in the middle when…

NEE–NAW! NEE–NAW!

Lights flashed, tyres screeched and Sergeant Snide roared past in his police car.

"Looks like Snidey's on a case," said Scratch.

"That he'll probably bungle again," said Sniff. "Let's go and see Penny."

The dogs bounded along the road to the police station.

Penny was standing outside, surrounded by traffic cones.

"I thought you boys might turn up," she said. "Inspector Hector's just told me there's been a robbery at Doogood's furniture store. As usual, Sergeant Snide's gone off to investigate by himself. He's left me here to count traffic cones. It's not fair!"

Scratch and Sniff looked at each other. Perhaps they could help Penny solve the crime.

"Looks like a case for the doggy Secret Service," said Scratch.

"Let's take the short cut to Doogood's furniture store and do some investigating ourselves," said Sniff.

Chapter Two

The dogs headed off down
neglected lanes and alleyways.

They dodged dirty dustbins, leapt
over litter, and outran cranky cats
till they arrived opposite
Doogood's furniture store.

They were
just in time to
see Sergeant
Snide march
up to the
entrance of the
shop, where
the manager
was waiting.

"I am
Sergeant
Snide," he bellowed, "and I can
spot a crook a mile away. Take me
to the crime scene immediately."

"Certainly," said the manager.
"Come this way."

Scratch and Sniff looked at each other.

"While the great detective is busy inside, shall we look around outside?" asked Scratch.

"Good idea," nodded Sniff. "We might be able to sniff out a few clues."

"We mustn't be seen, though," said Scratch. "I'll slither along on my belly."

"Mine nearly touches the ground anyway," said Sniff.

The dogs sneaked past the shop window and slipped round the corner to the back of the store. A large van was parked there. It had DOOGOOD'S FURNITURE written on the side.

Suddenly a door opened and two men in brown overalls came out carrying a sofa. They puffed and panted as they heaved it into the back of the van.

"That's strange," whispered Scratch. "Those men must work at Doogood's. But Snidey shouldn't be letting anyone go. He should be keeping them all inside for questioning."

"Snidey's brains are in his boots," muttered Sniff. "Let's take a closer look."

The dogs edged towards the van. They were just in time to hear the taller of the two men hiss: "Did you stash the money away safely, Bernie?"

"Stuffed it in the middle cushion, Stan," Bernie replied.

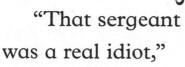

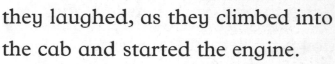

"That sergeant was a real idiot," they laughed, as they climbed into the cab and started the engine.

"They're the robbers!" gasped Scratch, "and they're getting away with the money!"

"We must do something," said Sniff.

Scratch and Sniff looked at each other.

"Cones!" they both barked.

Chapter Three

Scratch and Sniff headed back
down neglected lanes and
alleyways. They outran cranky
cats, leapt over litter, and dodged
dirty dustbins till they arrived at
the police station.

"Good," said Scratch. "The cones are still here. All we have to do is push one pile down the pavement to the junction and..."

"Block off the other road," agreed Sniff. "That way the Doogood's van will have to come down the High Street past the police station. But we must be quick, there's no time to lose."

The dogs hurried over to the nearest pile of cones.

"This will be easy," said Scratch. "When I was a champion sheep dog I was great at nudging sheep in the right direction."

"Then you can show me what to do," said Sniff. "I've only ever been a champion draught excluder."

Scratch nudged and pushed.

Sniff pushed and nudged.

Eventually the pile of cones reached the road junction. Then Sniff stepped off the pavement and held up a paw to stop the traffic, while Scratch toppled over the cones and lined them up across the road.

"Just look at those amazing dogs creating a diversion," said passers-by. "Whatever next!"

Scratch and Sniff hurried back to the police station. Penny was standing outside looking puzzled.

"There you are, boys," she said. "I was wondering where you'd gone. Have you seen a pile of cones? I seem to have lost..."

Then she saw that all the cars in the High Street had come to a halt.

"What's causing the traffic jam?" she wondered.

She was on her way to find out when she noticed the Doogood's van. "What's that doing here? Sergeant Snide shouldn't be allowing any vans to leave."

Scratch and Sniff looked at each other.

"Well done, Penny!" they both barked. "Good thinking!"

Chapter Four

Penny, followed by Scratch and Sniff, headed through the traffic jam to the Doogood's van.

The police constable rapped on the window.

"Can I have a word?" she said.

Bernie glanced at Stan, then rolled down the window.

"Certainly, Constable, how can I help you?"

"What are you carrying in your van?" asked Penny.

"Furniture," said Bernie. "See, it says so on the side of the van: DOOGOOD'S FURNITURE."

"That's the clue," giggled Stan.

"Could you open the back of your van, please?" said Penny. "I'd like to take a look."

"If you must, Constable," sighed Bernie. "But it's just furniture, and we're late for the delivery as it is."

Bernie and Stan got out and unlocked the back of the van.

"There you are," said Bernie. "One three-seater sofa to be delivered to Mrs Paterson, 4 Barnton Street."

Penny looked in the van. It was completely empty apart from the sofa. She climbed inside, walked all round the sofa, then peered underneath.

"There certainly doesn't seem to be anything out of place," she frowned.

"Then we'll be on our way, Constable," said Bernie.

"As soon as you've cleared the traffic jam," added Stan.

Penny started to get out of the van so Scratch and Sniff had to act quickly.

"We need to let Penny know what's in that middle cushion or the robbers will get away!" barked Scratch.

Sniff nodded. "That sofa looks very comfortable," he said. "Fancy a lie-down?"

Chapter Five

Scratch jumped up onto the sofa.

Sniff jumped and got his front paws onto the sofa.

"The rest of me will be along shortly, Scratch," he panted, as his back legs scrabbled up behind him.

"What are you two doing?" cried Penny. "Get down this minute!"

"Yeah, clear off, mutts," muttered Bernie.

Scratch and Sniff ignored him
and lay down.

"Scratch! Sniff! You'll ruin the
sofa with your dirty paws!" said
Penny.

"Dirty paws?" said Scratch.
"Then we'd better clean them
hadn't we, Sniff?"

And he began to scrape away
at the middle cushion.

Scrape. Scrape.

"Can't have dirty paws,"
agreed Sniff, and he joined in.

Scrape. Scrape.

Then they pushed the middle cushion onto the floor, and scraped at it again.

Scrape. Scrape.

"Control these dogs or we'll have the law on you, Constable," yelled Bernie and Stan.

"Be quiet!" said Penny. "I think the dogs are trying to tell me something…"

Scratch and Sniff looked at each other.

"The penny's dropped at last!" they barked.

Constable Penrose picked up the cushion and undid the back zip. Bundles of money fell out.

"Leg it, Stan!" cried Bernie. "The game's up!"

But Stan was already out of the van and running down the High Street.

Bernie followed close behind.

"They're getting away!" cried Penny. "After them!"

Scratch bounded after Stan and pulled him down. THUD! OW!

Sniff bounded after Bernie and tripped him up. THUD! OW!

Penny caught up with them all. She grabbed Bernie and Stan.

"You're nicked," she grinned and marched them back to the police station.

Sergeant Snide arrived just as
Penny was counting out the stolen
money.

"What's that?"
he demanded.

"The money from Doogood's
furniture shop," grinned Penny.
"Scratch and Sniff helped me
catch the robbers."

"And I'm taking Constable Penrose and the dogs to Mrs Pudding's cake shop to celebrate," said Inspector Hector.

Sergeant Snide glowered and stomped off.

"Congratulations on solving the case, Constable Penrose," said Inspector Hector, when they got to the cake shop.

"Thank you," blushed Penny. "But the credit should really go to Scratch and Sniff."

The doggy Secret Service barked and wagged their tails. They liked solving problems and now they had another: which delicious cake should they choose?

"I feel like a sticky bun," decided Scratch.

"That's funny," said Sniff. "You look like a collie!"

About the Author

Margaret Ryan lives in a creaky old mill and has red squirrels in her garden. She used to be a teacher, but gave up teaching because she didn't like sums.
She does like writing funny books, though, and you might like:
the *Airy Fairy* series, about an accident-prone little fairy. Or the *Fat Alphie and Charlie the Wimp* series, about two crazy alley cats. Or the *Littlest Dragon* series – imagine having nine older brothers!

Other White Wolves mystery
and adventure stories...

Michaela Morgan

As Scott passes the basement steps
of his new school, there's a bang
and a flash and a roaring sound.
Scott knows there's something
down there... something nasty...
something dangerous. What is it?
Can Scott piece together the
clues and solve the mystery?

The Thing in the Basement is a mystery
story in a school setting.

ISBN: 0-7136-7624-8   £4.99

Year 3

Detective Dan • Vivian French

Buffalo Bert, the Cowboy Grandad • Michaela Morgan

Treasure at the Boot-fair • Chris Powling

Scratch and Sniff • Margaret Ryan

The Thing in the Basement • Michaela Morgan

On the Ghost Trail • Chris Powling

Year 4

Hugo and the Long Red Arm • Rachel Anderson

Live the Dream • Jenny Oldfield

Swan Boy • Diana Hendry

Taking Flight • Julia Green

Finding Fizz • J. Alexander

Nothing But Trouble • Alan MacDonald

Other White Wolves mystery
and adventure stories...

ON THE
GHOST
TRAIL

Chris Powling

There are signs of a ghost in
Grandpas's creaky old house. Bits of
it have been left in the chimney and
you can hear its heartbeat at night.
So when Adam dares his brother and
sister to get on the ghost trail and
hunt it down in the graveyard at
midnight, who will be brave
enough to go with him?

On the Ghost Trail is a spooky mystery.

ISBN: 0-7136-7680-9   £4.99